KIDS CAN'T STOP READING THE CHOOSE YOUR OWN ADVENTURE® STORIES!

"Choose Your Own Adventure is the best thing that has come along since books themselves."

—Alysha Beyer, age 11

"I didn't read much before, but now I read my Choose Your Own Adventure books almost every night."

—Chris Brogan, age 13

"I love the control I have over what happens next."

—Kosta Efstathiou, age 17

"Choose Your Own Adventure books are so much fun to read and collect—I want them all!"

—Brendan Davin, age 11

And teachers like this series, too:

"We have read and reread, worn thin, loved, loaned, bought for others, and donated to school libraries our Choose Your Own Adventure books."

CHOOSE YOUR OWN ADVENTURE®— AND MAKE READING MORE FUN!

Bantam Books in the Choose Your Own Adventure® Series
Ask your bookseller for the books you have missed

#1 THE CAVE OF TIME
#2 JOURNEY UNDER THE SEA
#3 BY BALLOON TO THE SAHARA
#4 SPACE AND BEYOND
#5 THE MYSTERY OF CHIMNEY ROCK
#6 YOUR CODE NAME IS JONAH
#7 THE THIRD PLANET FROM ALTAIR
#8 DEADWOOD CITY
#9 WHO KILLED HARLOWE THROMBEY?
#10 THE LOST JEWELS OF NABOOTI
#11 MYSTERY OF THE MAYA
#12 INSIDE UFO 54 40
#13 THE ABOMINABLE SNOWMAN
#14 THE FORBIDDEN CASTLE
#15 HOUSE OF DANGER
#16 SURVIVAL AT SEA
#17 THE RACE FOREVER
#18 UNDERGROUND KINGDOM
#19 SECRET OF THE PYRAMIDS
#20 ESCAPE
#21 HYPERSPACE
#22 SPACE PATROL
#23 THE LOST TRIBE
#24 LOST ON THE AMAZON
#25 PRISONER OF THE ANT PEOPLE
#26 THE PHANTOM SUBMARINE
#27 THE HORROR OF HIGH RIDGE
#28 MOUNTAIN SURVIVAL
#29 TROUBLE ON PLANET EARTH
#30 THE CURSE OF BATTERSLEA HALL
#31 VAMPIRE EXPRESS
#32 TREASURE DIVER
#33 THE DRAGONS' DEN
#34 THE MYSTERY OF THE HIGHLAND CREST
#35 JOURNEY TO STONEHENGE
#36 THE SECRET TREASURE OF TIBET
#37 WAR WITH THE EVIL POWER MASTER
#38 SABOTAGE
#39 SUPERCOMPUTER
#40 THE THRONE OF ZEUS
#41 SEARCH FOR THE MOUNTAIN GORILLAS
#42 THE MYSTERY OF ECHO LODGE
#43 GRAND CANYON ODYSSEY
#44 THE MYSTERY OF URA SENKE
#45 YOU ARE A SHARK
#46 THE DEADLY SHADOW
#47 OUTLAWS OF SHERWOOD FOREST
#48 SPY FOR GEORGE WASHINGTON
#49 DANGER AT ANCHOR MINE
#50 RETURN TO THE CAVE OF TIME
#51 THE MAGIC OF THE UNICORN
#52 GHOST HUNTER
#53 THE CASE OF THE SILK KING
#54 FOREST OF FEAR
#55 THE TRUMPET OF TERROR

CHOOSE YOUR OWN ADVENTURE® • 55

THE TRUMPET OF TERROR

BY DEBORAH LERME GOODMAN

ILLUSTRATED BY TED ENIK

An R. A. Montgomery Book

BANTAM BOOKS
TORONTO • NEW YORK • LONDON • SYDNEY • AUCKLAND

RL 4, IL age 10 and up

THE TRUMPET OF TERROR
A Bantam Book / April 1986

CHOOSE YOUR OWN ADVENTURE® is a registered trademark of Bantam Books, Inc. Registered in U. S. Patent and Trademark Office and elsewhere.

Original conception of Edward Packard

ISBN 0-553-25491-X

Published simultaneously in the United States and Canada

Bantam Books are published by Bantam Books, Inc. Its trademark, consisting of the words "Bantam Books" and the portrayal of a rooster, is Registered in U. S. Patent and Trademark Office and in other countries. Marca Registrada. Bantam Books, Inc., 666 Fifth Avenue, New York, New York 10103.

PRINTED IN THE UNITED STATES OF AMERICA

O 0 9 8 7 6 5 4 3 2 1

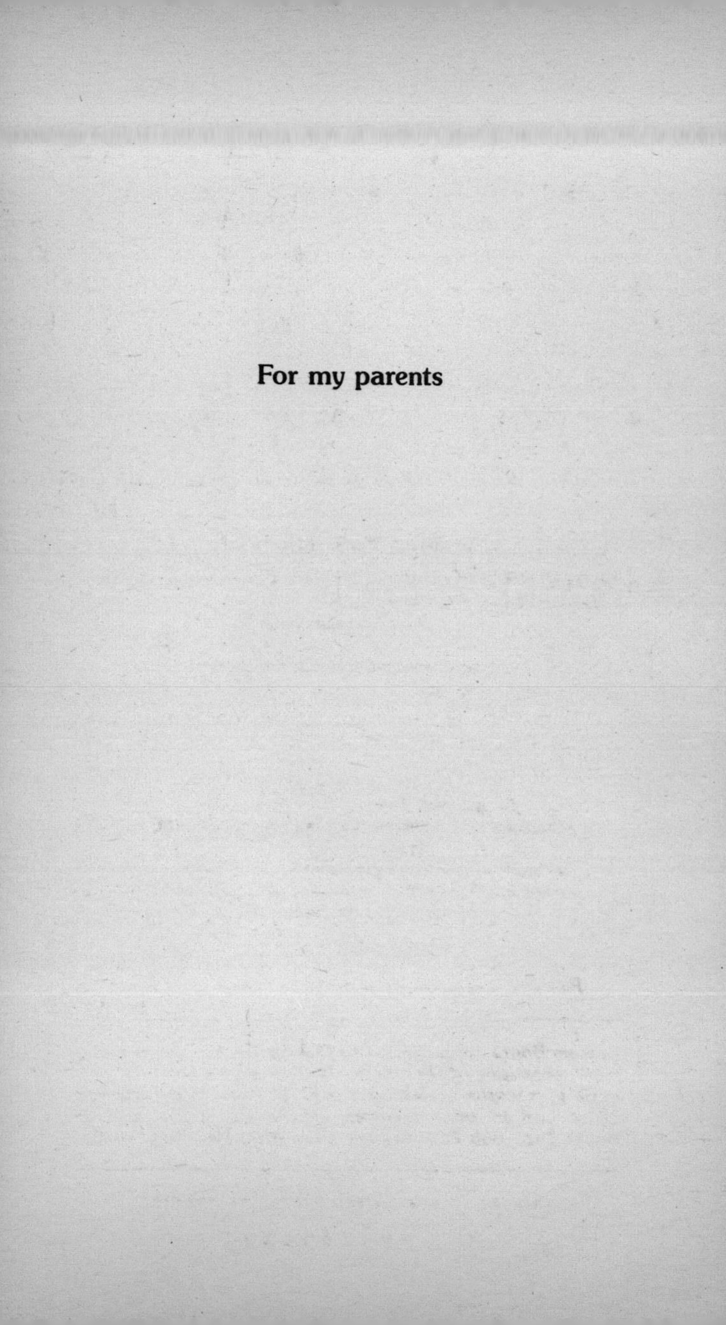

For my parents

Norse Names Used in This Book

Aegir (EYE-geer) A giant, lord of the stormy seas.
Aesir (EYE-zeer) One group of gods in Norse mythology.
Alfheim (ALF-heim) The home of the elves.
Asgard (AS-gard) The home of the Aesir gods.
Frigg (frig) Odin's wife and the highest-ranking Aesir goddess.
Gna (naw) One of Frigg's ladies-in-waiting.
Gullveig (GULE-vay) A witch from Vanaheim who came to Asgard looking for gold.
Heimdall (HIME-dahl) One of Odin's sons, who stood guard at the top of the rainbow bridges to Asgard.
Hel (hell) One of Loki's daughters; she ruled the underworld.
Idunn (EE-doon) The goddess who kept the golden apples that made the Aesir gods immortal.
Jotunheim (YOH-tun-hime) The cold and mountainous home of the frost giants.
Loki (LOH-kee) A mischievous and sometimes evil character who was Odin's blood-brother, although not an Aesir god.
Midgard (MID-gard) The earth, the home of human beings.
Mimir (MEE-meer) A friendly giant; he was beheaded by the Vanir gods, but Odin revived his head and placed it by the Well of Wisdom.
Muspellheim (MOOS-pel-hime) The home of fire demons.

Nithog (NITH-og) A winged dragon that lived in the Cloud River in Asgard.

Norns (norns) Three sisters who spun a thread of fate for every human being, god, and goddess.

Odin (OH-din) The one-eyed father of the Aesir gods.

Sif (seef) Thor's wife; she was the goddess of the home and family.

Sleipnir (SLEYEP-neer) Odin's eight-legged horse.

Thor (thor) The strongest of the Aesir gods and one of Odin's sons. He carried a powerful hammer, and wore a magic belt that increased his strength.

Valhalla (VAL-hal-ah) A vast hall in Asgard where Odin's army lived.

Valkyries (VAL-keer-eez) Warrior maidens who carried slain heroes to Valhalla.

Vanaheim (VAN-ah-hime) The home of the Vanir gods.

Vanir (VAH-neer) Another group of Norse gods and goddesses.

Yggdrasil (EEG-drah-zill) An enormous ash tree that grew in the middle of the universe, supporting the many worlds of Norse mythology.

WARNING!!!

Do not read this book straight through from beginning to end! These pages contain many different adventures you can have with the Norse gods in the age of the Vikings. As you read along you will be asked to make decisions and choices. The adventures you have will be the result of the decisions you make. *You* are responsible because *you* choose! After you make a choice, follow the instructions to see what happens next.

Think carefully before you make a move. You alone have the power to help the Norse gods . . . but only if you choose wisely.

SPECIAL WARNING!!!

Before you begin your adventures, you may want to know more about the place you'll be visiting. The information on the next page will provide you with a background in Norse mythology. If you decide to read it, you should be well prepared for the realm of the Norse gods!

ASGARD
ALFHEIM
VANAHEIM
JOTUNHEIM
MIDGARD
GNOMES AND DWARVES
MUSPELLHEIM
UNDERWORLD
YGGDRASIL

Special Information for This Book

Hundreds and hundreds of years ago, during the age of the Vikings, the people of Scandinavia believed that an enormous ash tree called Yggdrasil supported the universe. Within this universe were many different worlds.

Midgard was the most familiar of them because it was where human beings lived. Next to Midgard was Jotunheim, the icy home of the frost giants. Gnomes and dwarfs lived in their own land under the earth. And even farther below, beyond the roots of Yggdrasil, were two more worlds: Muspellheim, home of the fire demons, and the underworlds ruled by the grotesque goddess Hel.

Within the many branches of Yggdrasil were Alfheim—the land of the elves—and Vanaheim, the home of the Vanir gods. Between these two worlds and the highest heaven was Asgard, home of the Aesir gods and goddesses.

Radiant rainbow bridges connected Asgard and Midgard. Human beings could not normally ascend the bridges, but they were well traveled by the Aesir. Odin, the one-eyed father of this clan, took a special interest in earthly events.

After a visit to Midgard, Odin would ride back to Asgard on Sleipnir, his eight-legged horse. At the top of the rainbow he would greet his son Heimdall, the gatekeeper. Then he would hurry on to see his wife, Frigg.

Sometimes Odin spotted trouble in Midgard. More often than not, this was the work of Loki,

Odin's evil blood brother. Fortunately Odin was able to solve most of these problems with the help of his most powerful son, Thor. A mighty hammer and a strength-increasing belt made Thor nearly invincible.

The Aesir gods and goddesses enjoyed perfect health and even immortality, thanks to magical golden apples tended by the goddess Idunn. Life in Asgard was happy and full of celebrations—until now. Gullveig, a beautiful but evil witch, has come to visit and has decided to stay. Troubles multiply so quickly that Odin cannot handle them, even with Thor's help. He realizes he has to seek aid outside Asgard. There is only one human being he can turn to, and it is you.

All your life you've waited eagerly for your first ocean voyage. And on this summer morning in 938, you are finally setting sail for Iceland from the bustling Danish port of Sandeborg.

As you help the crew load the last of the supplies on the longship, your friend Nils comments, "We're lucky the captain is giving us this chance to row with the men."

You nod your head in agreement. "Ever since I inherited Odin's Trumpet of Terror from my father, I've had good luck." You glance proudly at the curved golden horn hanging from your belt. A long time ago Odin, father of the gods, presented it to your great-grandfather as a symbol of your family's wisdom and courage.

Turn to page 2.

2

Nils watches you enviously. "That trumpet must be great in battle. Just imagine—you blow that horn and your enemies are so frightened by the sound that they surrender immediately! Why don't you blow it right now and see what happens?"

"Nils!" you exclaim. "I can blow the Trumpet of Terror only *once*! I have to save it for a serious emergency! Now, let's go. We're the only ones who aren't on board."

As you make your way along the crowded dock you see a tall man wearing a blue cloak spangled with thousands of silver stars. To your surprise you notice he is staring at you intently with a single piercing eye. With a shiver you recall that Odin has only one eye.

Turn to page 5.

"All right," says Odin. "You'll find the Norns by the root of Yggdrasil. I'll show you how to get there." Odin leads you to two rainbow bridges at the edge of Asgard. There you see a god dressed entirely in white, from his boots to his winged helmet. He waves to you and Odin.

"This is my son Heimdall, guardian of our rainbow bridges," Odin tells you. To Heimdall he explains, "My young friend from Midgard is going to ask the Norns to change the fate of Gullveig. I know we don't allow human beings to travel the bridge there, but you'll have to make an exception today."

Heimdall strokes his snowy beard. "This is our most fragile bridge. It is merely light and vapor. I doubt anyone but a god or goddess could safely tread on it."

"Is there any other way to the Norns?" you ask.

"Well, yes," says Heimdall. "You could try rafting down the Cloud River. But I must warn you—it is more turbulent than any you've ever seen. What's more, it's full of shards of ice that will slice you to ribbons if you fall in the water."

Odin nervously twists his gnarled hands. "Both routes have their share of danger. Thank Yggdrasil, you have the Trumpet of Terror to help you."

If you tell Odin you'll cross this rainbow bridge, turn to page 23.

If you decide to try your luck on the Cloud River, turn to page 15.

You grab Nils by the shoulder. "Do you see that man watching me? I think he may be Odin!"

Nils glares at you with exasperation. "Ever since you got that horn, you've thought you were special. But there's no reason Odin would care so much about you. Besides, that man looks too weary to be a god."

Just as you decide Nils must be right, the one-eyed stranger beckons you. You freeze in your tracks.

"Hurry up!" cries Nils. "The captain won't wait much longer for us!"

If you answer, "All right, I'm coming,"
turn to page 80.

If you tell Nils, "Go on without me. I want to find out if that man is really Odin,"
turn to page 9.

"You see," Odin continues, "the goddess Idunn feeds us magical golden apples that prevent us from aging. Gullveig has made Idunn so unhappy that she's fled Asgard and taken the apples with her. Now we're all growing old with alarming speed."

Odin snaps the reins, and Sleipnir breaks into a gallop. You try to keep track of the path you take, but the countryside whizzes by in a blur. Finally, Sleipnir comes to a halt at the base of a vast, radiant rainbow.

"This is a bridge between Midgard, your world, and Asgard," says Odin.

With a lurch Sleipnir dashes up the rainbow. He stops in a broad green plain gleaming with golden palaces.

"How beautiful!" you exclaim. "I can't wait to explore Asgard!" You slide off Sleipnir.

"There's no time to waste!" Odin reminds you sternly. "Each day we grow older!"

"Should I look for Idunn and the apples first, or should I try to lure Gullveig away?" you ask.

Odin shrugs wearily. "My mind is muddled. Do whatever you think is best."

If you decide to search for Idunn before doing anything else, turn to page 10.

If you think it's best to get rid of Gullveig first, turn to page 29.

"I'll follow you," you tell the falcon.

The journey takes hours. Finally you reach a remote region of stark cliffs and ravines, and the falcon leads you to a deep black hole. Gusts of snowflakes are swirling out of the opening.

"Idunn is hiding down there," says the falcon. "You go first and I'll fly right behind."

You soar down into the chasm. It takes a few seconds for your eyes to adjust to the darkness, and a few more seconds to get over your surprise. At the bottom of the hole is an enormous wolf!

"Idunn *can't* be down there!" you shout.

"Don't mind the wolf," says the falcon.

Sure enough, the wolf lets you and the falcon go by, then quickly blocks the passageway again. You step out of the passageway and find yourself facing a gloomy castle surrounded by craggy mountains and ice-clotted rivers.

When you turn to ask the falcon where you are, you discover a handsome man standing in its place. "Wh-who are you?" you stammer.

"I'm Loki," he answers, and your stomach sinks. All your life you've heard tales of Loki's evil adventures, but you never thought you'd be caught up in one yourself! "My daughter Hel, queen of the underworld, will make sure you stay here forever!" He continues, "Your days of meddling are over."

"Meddling? Who's meddling?" you ask, challenging Loki.

But Loki doesn't answer. Instead, he turns into a falcon again and flies away.

Turn to page 68.

You walk over to the stranger. Gazing into his single eye, you whisper, "Are you Odin?"

"Yes," he replies, "and I need your help desperately. There is serious trouble in Asgard, home of the gods. We've tried everything we can think of to solve the problem. Please come—you're my last hope."

"Me?" You can hardly believe your ears!

"Your family has always been as clever as it is courageous," Odin tells you. "What's more, *you* are the bravest and brightest of all. No other human being can help the gods. Will you come with me?"

You nod solemnly.

Turn to page 11.

"I think I'd better find Idunn first," you tell Odin. "Do you have any idea where I should begin my search?"

Odin shakes his head woefully. "Idunn is very fond of swimming, so you could look at the lakes and ponds. But I must tell you, we've done some searching on our own, and she seems to have vanished completely."

"It could take me *years* to search for Idunn if I have to go all over the world on foot," you say. "Could you give me some kind of power that would help me travel more quickly?"

Odin hesitates. "Ordinarily I don't like to offer human beings any of the magical powers of the gods. It makes them vain."

"You gave my great-grandfather your Trumpet of Terror," you remind him.

"That's right," says Odin, "and I'll make another exception for you. Let's see, I could ask my son Thor to take you in his chariot, or perhaps you could borrow my wife Frigg's falcon suit so you could fly by yourself."

You've heard countless stories about the mighty Thor; you're eager to meet him and see his strength-increasing belt. But you also love the idea of being able to fly.

If you decide to go with Thor, turn to page 33.

If you'd rather fly by yourself, turn to page 18.

Odin leads you away from the harbor and explains, "As you know, I am the father of the Aesir gods. Our neighbors, the Vanir gods, are generally friendly, but one of them, an evil witch named Gullveig, has made herself at home in Asgard. She was our guest at first, but now she won't leave. She's making the Aesir gods miserable! We have to wait on her, dance for her, even give her our gold. We've all become sad and tired, worried and sick."

"You can't force her to leave?" you ask.

He shakes his head. "She has a power over us, and besides, we don't dare offend the Vanir. If we resort to violence, there's no telling how they will react. I don't want to risk our peaceful relations."

"I understand," you reply.

You reach the edge of town and find an eight-legged horse tied to a tree.

"I'm afraid you'll have to climb up on Sleipnir yourself," says Odin. "I'm too weak to lift you. Oh, I hate getting old!"

You mount the horse and help Odin up. "I thought you were immortal," you tell him.

Odin sighs ruefully. "None of the gods is truly immortal."

Turn to page 6.

12

Odin leads you to a courtyard where three goddesses are dancing for a tall blond witch—Gullveig. You are surprised to find she is almost as pretty as the goddesses. It is not until you look more closely that you see a glint of cruelty in her eyes.

Gullveig laughs shrilly and shouts, "Faster! Faster!"

"We're tired!" the goddesses complain. Their feet drag on the ground.

"Why don't the goddesses just stop dancing?" you whisper to Odin.

"They are powerless," he explains. "As long as Gullveig is in Asgard, she can cast spells to control us. She can make us do almost anything she wants."

Turn to page 14.

You turn back to Gullveig, who is now shouting, "Sif, toss me your earrings! Gna, I want that bracelet!"

"I've never met anyone so greedy for gold!" Odin tells you. "Gullveig has already taken most of our coins and jewelry."

"That gives me an idea!" you exclaim. "Actually, it gives me *two* ideas! If we had a golden boat, I could offer Gullveig a ride on it and sail her out of Asgard. Do you have a golden boat?"

"No," Odin replies, "but you might be able to get the underground dwarfs to make you one. They are ill-tempered creatures, unpleasant to deal with, but they are master goldsmiths. What's your other idea?"

"I've heard there's a wizard in Lapland who creates enchanted carpets. He can make rugs that fly and rugs that float. Maybe he could weave a golden rug to carry Gullveig out of Asgard."

"That sounds promising!" says Odin.

You nod. "Of course, finding the Lapland wizard won't be easy. For all I know, he might be just a myth."

Odin spreads his hands. "Either idea is worth a try."

If you decide to go to the dwarfs for help, turn to page 20.

If you want to look for the Lapland wizard, turn to page 34.

"If you can give me a sturdy raft, I'll take my chances on the Cloud River," you tell Odin and Heimdall.

"Then come with me," says Odin. You say good-bye to Heimdall and follow Odin to a boathouse. You stare in awe at a dozen dragon ships and are a little disappointed when Odin gives you just what you requested—a sturdy but ordinary raft.

The Cloud River runs past the boathouse. You have seen turbulent water before, but nothing like this river! The water glistens with silvery slivers of ice as it crashes over jagged rocks.

Go on to the next page.

"Do you have any advice?" you ask Odin nervously.

He shakes his head. "Just hold on tight and keep your hands out of the water. Those bits of ice are as sharp as knives." Odin steadies the raft as you climb on.

Before you can say good-bye, the raging current sweeps you away from Asgard. You clutch the raft with all your might. The waves toss you from side to side, but you manage to hang on. Just when you think you've passed the worst of the rapids, you notice that the Cloud River forks in three directions ahead.

Turn to page 19.

"Will Frigg lend me her falcon suit?" you ask Odin.

"Of course," he answers. "Let's go to her palace."

The two of you walk toward one of the largest palaces in Asgard. Inside you find many goddesses spinning and weaving. "They're making summer clouds," Odin explains.

He introduces you to Frigg, a beautiful goddess with sorrowful eyes and long blond braids streaked with silver. Odin describes your mission and asks her to lend you her falcon suit.

"Certainly," replies Frigg. She opens a wooden chest and removes a large winged costume made of feathers. You eye it skeptically as she fluffs up the feathers and brushes off some dust.

"Will I really be able to fly in this suit?" you ask.

"Yes!" say Odin and Frigg, laughing. They drape it over you, fitting your arms into the wings. As Frigg lowers the headpiece over your face you feel a tingling sensation in your bones.

"You're all set," says Odin.

You thank Frigg, then follow Odin outside.

"Just flap your wings," he tells you.

Turn to page 62.

Why didn't Odin tell you about this? you wonder. Quickly you study the three branches of the river for clues. To the left you see a pale-green mist hovering above the icy waves. To the right the sky glows with a cool white light. And straight ahead the river looks calm; the sky is blue. Which is the way to the Norns?

If you lean your weight to the left,
turn to page 54.

If you try to swing the raft to the right,
turn to page 24.

If you float straight ahead, turn to page 46.

"How do I reach the dwarfs?" you ask Odin.

"There is an underground passage between Asgard and the land of gnomes and dwarfs," Odin explains. He leads you to a stairway that winds away below you. Handing you a torch, he says, "Go down the steps and follow the tunnel. Good luck!"

You say good-bye, then make your way underground. The torch casts spooky shadows on the walls. You reach the bottom of the steps and enter the tunnel.

After walking several miles, you hear the clinking of hammers. You round a bend in the tunnel and find yourself in a workshop full of small people with bulging eyes and large noses. They are banging away on pieces of gold.

Turn to page 28.

"I've come to see the work you do," you tell the Norns. "Will you show me how you spin?" You want to gain their confidence before you ask a favor.

The sisters huddle together. Their voices buzz softly but you can't understand a word they say. The relentless hum unnerves you.

Finally one of the Norns tells you, "No one has ever asked to see our spinning before, but we think it's all right to show you." Each of the women picks up a golden spindle and twists some gray fibers into slender, silvery threads.

"Is that wool?" you ask, pointing to the fibers.

"Oh, no," replies one sister. "That is the stuff of dreams and danger, hopes and hardship, wishes and war. You can't spin fate from ordinary wool!"

"Each thread is someone's life," explains another Norn. "Some are strong, others are fragile. We spin some threads that seem to go on forever, while others we snip short. We twine some lives together neatly and tangle others with tight knots."

"Could you show me the thread of Gullveig's fate?" you ask.

Turn to page 30.

"If I make it to the end of the rainbow bridge, how will I know where to find the Norns?" you ask Odin and Heimdall.

"At the end of the bridge you'll see a well that glows like the moon. You should find three women nearby with shawls draped over their faces. They are the Norns," says Odin. "You'll recognize them right away."

You have a feeling it won't be that easy.

"And keep an eye out for the eagle," warns Heimdall.

"What eagle?" You try not to sound alarmed.

Odin groans. "I forgot about that ornery beast. It sits at the top of Yggdrasil watching over the universe. Normally the eagle leaves us alone, but it may not like the idea of a human traveling across the bridge to the Norns."

"Well," says Heimdall without much hope, "just do your best."

Turn to page 32.

You shift your weight, and the raft gradually swerves to the right. A swift current carries you toward the softly glowing light.

Before long you pass a clearing. There you see three women shrouded in gray shawls, drawing water from a large well. They must be the Norns! you tell yourself.

You grab onto a tree that bends over the river and scramble through the branches to shore. The raft floats away down the Cloud River without you.

As you walk toward the Norns you hear a faint high-pitched hum. You're not sure why, but the sound sends shivers up your spine.

"Hello!" you call to the three sisters. The humming noise stops abruptly. They whirl around to face you.

Except for their soft gray eyes and slender hands, the Norns are draped with layers and layers of filmy cloth. They look pale and shadowy.

"Why have you come here?" asks one sister in a strange, droning voice.

Turn to page 22.

As soon as you try to twist Gullveig's thread of fate in a different way, it becomes tangled with thousands of other threads. The Norns struggle to tear the yarn out of your hands, but they only succeed in making the snarls worse.

The lives of human beings, gods, goddesses, giants, and demons are hopelessly twisted. Even the nimble fingers of the Norns can't undo the knots.

The three sisters weep softly as they examine the mess. "The universe is in chaos now!" exclaims one. "A young lad from Sandeborg named Nils has become father of the gods, and Odin is now a cobbler in Hedeby!"

"Look!" cries another Norn. "Ships are now steered by captains who have never before laid eyes on the sea! Whole nations are ruled by milkmaids and stableboys!"

The third sister pulls at an especially tangled piece of yarn and glares at you. "This is the thread of *your* fate. When you return to Midgard, you will try to tell people about your adventure here, but no one will believe you. They will think you are a fool. You are destined to be the village idiot."

The End

You run faster than you thought possible, but the giant eagle looms right behind you. With one quick lunge it pierces your tunic with its talons. To your horror you find yourself being lifted high above the rainbow.

Helplessly you gaze down. Beyond the radiant bridge you see three women shrouded in gray shawls. A large well glows softly beside them. The Norns! If you can just reach them, maybe they'll protect you from the eagle.

You writhe and wriggle, trying to free yourself. And suddenly you are plummeting through the air with alarming speed.

Splash! You plunge straight into the Norns' well. Choking on the cold water, you struggle to the surface.

Three heads swathed in filmy gray cloth appear at the edge of the well. Only their eyes—the color of mist—are visible. Clucking anxiously, they help you climb out. To your surprise your wet hair and clothes dry instantly.

You glance fearfully at the eagle, hovering high above.

"Don't worry, it won't bother you here," says one of the Norns in a low voice.

"The eagle cares only about the bridge," says another sister.

"Where were you going?" asks the third.

Turn to page 22.

You introduce yourself to one of the dwarfs and tell him about Gullveig. "Could you make a golden boat to carry her out of Asgard?" you ask.

"Yes, but it will cost you a handsome sum," says the dwarf crossly.

You groan. You didn't bring anything to trade. "Do you have a golden boat I could just borrow?"

The dwarf eyes you suspiciously. "As it happens, we do. But how do I know you'll return it?"

"I'll leave my golden trumpet with you. If I don't return your boat by tomorrow, you can keep my horn."

The dwarf scratches his pointed ear. "Sounds fair enough."

He leads you to a small but beautiful golden boat. It is just big enough for you and Gullveig.

You hand the dwarf the Trumpet of Terror, then wonder aloud, "How am I ever going to get this boat back to Asgard?"

"We'll help you if you'll give us two fistfuls of gold once we get there," says the dwarf. You agree, and he rounds up several of his friends. Together you carry the boat through the tunnel and up the stairs to Asgard.

Odin is waiting by the steps, wringing his hands. "I thought you'd never get here! Gullveig is driving me mad! Please hurry!"

Turn to page 89.

"I'll try to think of a way to lure Gullveig out of Asgard," you tell Odin. "Do you have any suggestions?"

Odin sighs with exasperation. "If I had suggestions, I wouldn't have asked you for help in the first place!" He rubs his brow. "Those cursed Norns! It's all their fault."

"Who are the Norns?" you ask.

"They are three sisters who spin the threads of fate for gods and human beings alike," he answers. "If only they'd spun more carefully, we probably wouldn't have this problem!"

"Do you think the Norns could spin Gullveig's destiny again?" you ask.

"I don't know," says Odin. "It's been two or three years since I've had to deal with those sisters. They've never taken kindly to my suggestions. Why don't I show you Gullveig? Maybe after you've seen her, you'll think of something."

If you say, "I'd like to try to persuade the Norns to help us get rid of Gullveig," *turn to page 4.*

If you tell Odin, "I'd like to see Gullveig for myself," *turn to page 12.*

The Norns murmur among themselves, then begin sorting through skeins of thread. "Here," says one sister, handing you the end of a long, sturdy piece of yarn.

"Gullveig is making the Aesir gods miserable," you explain. "Would it be possible for you to re-spin her fate so she won't interfere in Asgard?"

"Impossible! We never change what we spin!" they chorus.

"Please?" you cry. You can't believe you've risked your life for nothing.

"Never!"

You realize you'll have to change Gullveig's thread of fate yourself—and quickly, before they take back the yarn.

If you try to respin Gullveig's thread of fate, turn to page 25.

If you decide to cut the thread in half with your knife, turn to page 39.

You say good-bye to the gods, then gingerly step onto the shimmering rainbow bridge. To your relief you don't fall through the soft colors. You move quickly and lightly, like a deer, hoping you won't step on any weak spots.

Suddenly a vast shadow crosses your path. Looking up, you see a gigantic eagle—bigger than a horse—swiftly descending toward you. You gasp at the sight of its powerful talons. You know you must act fast. Is there time to unhook the Trumpet of Terror from your belt and blow it? Will the trumpet even frighten a giant eagle? Maybe you should just run for your life!

If you try to blow the Trumpet of Terror, turn to page 90.

If you race away from the eagle, turn to page 26.

"I'll go with Thor," you tell Odin.

Odin introduces you to his red-bearded son. Thor shakes your hand, practically crushing the bones. You remind yourself that he wears a magic belt that multiplies his strength. With that belt and his mighty hammer Thor is the most powerful being in Asgard.

"Wait till you see my chariot!" exclaims Thor. "It's drawn by the biggest goats you've ever seen—Toothgnasher and Toothgrinder! We'll find Idunn quickly enough." He lifts you onto his shoulders and carries you to his gleaming silver chariot. Odin waves good-bye.

Thor places you in the chariot, climbs in beside you, and snaps the reins. You're off. Deafening thunder roars beneath the wheel. Lightning flashes! You are breathless with excitement.

You spend nearly a week searching through Midgard. Shortly before you reach a group of lakes Idunn has always liked, you come to a towering wall of flames. Thor halts the chariot and shouts, "What's this? The fire demons of Muspellheim must be invading!"

Turn to page 40.

"I'll try to find the Lapland wizard," you tell Odin, "but I'm not sure where to start. Do you have any ideas?"

Odin strokes his beard. "I'll let you look at the universe from my throne. You can see everything from there. Maybe you'll be able to spot the wizard."

The view from Odin's throne is spectacular! You can see lands you never knew existed. You search carefully for the wizard.

"I see him!" you cry at last. "There's a little man surrounded by some bright rugs. I'm sure he's the wizard."

You point the wizard out to Odin. While he is looking toward Lapland, your gaze wanders to your hometown, Sandeborg.

You gaze fondly at your street. Then you look at the harbor to see which ships are in. You are just scanning the ocean to see if you can spot Nils sailing to Iceland when you notice an enormous tidal wave! Even though it is still far out at sea, it is headed straight for your hometown!

Go on to the next page.

"Look!" you shriek. "That tidal wave is going to hit Sandeborg! I have to warn everyone!"

"Wait," says Odin. "Disasters happen every day. There's nothing you can do about it."

"I know I can't stop the wave, but if we hurry, we can at least warn my family and my neighbors!" you retort.

"Which do you think is more important in the long run—getting Gullveig out of Asgard or telling your friends about an unavoidable tidal wave?" Odin asks you sternly.

If you agree that the most important thing you can do now is lure Gullveig from Asgard, turn to page 84.

If you insist on warning your village, turn to page 65.

"I'd rather look for Idunn myself," you tell the falcon. "Thank you anyway."

"You'll never find her," the bird replies snidely.

After days of searching you begin to worry that the falcon is right. But then you come to an especially pretty lake and stop to look for the goddess. You don't see her, but you decide to go for a swim. You remove the falcon suit and wade into the water.

You splash around for a while before noticing that the water is remarkably clear. You swim to the center of the lake to find out if you can see the bottom out there too.

You can't believe your eyes! Far below is a woman with long hair streaming out in all directions. You immediately dive down, hoping it is not too late to save her. It is not until you grab her shoulder that you spot the golden apples in a basket beside her.

Turn to page 44.

"I'll give up my eye," you tell Mimir. "But how?"

"Simply pluck it out with your fingers. It's much easier than you would imagine," he answers.

The pain is less awful than you expected, but you still feel queasy. You quickly distract yourself with a long drink from the Well of Wisdom.

The water tastes ordinary, but gradually you sense a buzzing in your head as your brain struggles to accommodate all the thoughts rushing in. In a matter of minutes you know not one but eight or nine ways to lure Gullveig out of Asgard. You even know a safe route back to Odin.

Back in Asgard you tell Odin, "I have all kinds of ideas for getting rid of Gullveig. We could trick her with a false message from the Vanir gods begging her to come home. We could create a treasure hunt for her that leads out of Asgard. Or—"

"Wait!" cries Odin. "These are wonderful schemes but what about Idunn?"

"She's hiding at the bottom of Crystal Lake outside Asarna," you reply.

Sure enough, Gullveig hurries out of Asgard as soon as she reads the letter she believes to be from the Vanir. When she is safely out of sight, you go to Midgard to retrieve Idunn and the golden apples. Odin thanks you profusely, then you go home.

You are soon recognized as the wisest person in all of Europe. You cure diseases, help farmers improve their harvests, and even predict the future. Kings and queens come from far and wide to ask your advice. Philosophers and alchemists seek your opinion. You are famous!

The End

Without a moment's hesitation you grab your knife and deftly slice Gullveig's thread of fate in half.

The Norns gasp with horror. They snatch the two pieces of yarn back and study them intently. Then, turning their backs to you, the sisters begin to laugh with low, eerie voices.

"What's so funny?" you shout. "I was only trying to help Odin!"

One of the Norns looks over her shoulder at you and giggles. "You haven't helped Odin at all! You've created *two* Gullveigs—and twice as much trouble!"

The End

Although the heat of the flames reddens your face, you find yourself shivering with fear.

Suddenly Thor is engulfed by fire. He tumbles out of the chariot. To your shock you realize he is being attacked by three blazing demons!

"Your hammer!" you call to him. "Hit them with your hammer!"

"It won't work! These monsters are made of nothing but fire!" he cries.

Is there time to drive the chariot back to Asgard to get help? you wonder. Or would the Trumpet of Terror scare the fire demons away? You must do something—fast!

If you turn the chariot around and head toward Asgard, turn to page 74.

If you raise the Trumpet of Terror to your lips, turn to page 98.

You can think of only one way to make the frost giant let go of you. You bite his finger as hard as you can.

"Owww!" he screams, releasing you.

You immediately raise the Trumpet of Terror to your mouth and blow with all your might. It makes a horrifying sound. The two frost giants clutch each other with fear. Then they race away from you.

You stand there, marveling at the power of the trumpet. Soon you hear the clatter of hooves. You turn quickly, fearing it is a frost giant on horseback, but to your relief you see that it is Odin riding Sleipnir.

"I heard the trumpet," he explains. "I came as quickly as I could."

You tell him about the Cloud River, Mimir, and the giants.

"You've had enough trouble for one day," says Odin sympathetically. "Climb up on Sleipnir and I'll give you a ride to Asgard. You can continue your search tomorrow."

The End

The goddess Idunn is very much alive. You try to pull her toward the surface, but she struggles. When you are almost out of breath, you finally reach the surface of the lake.

"The gods need you!" you tell her between gulps of air. "They need your apples. They're losing their immortality."

"I'm sorry," she replies, "but I don't want to go back. Living in Asgard is awful when Gullveig is there. Besides, I've come to like living underwater."

"But the gods will die without your help!"

Idunn smooths her wet hair. "If you go back to Asgard and tell Odin you can't find me anywhere, I'll give you an apple to keep yourself. It will last for centuries if you nibble it carefully."

You know Odin is counting on you to bring back Idunn, but you could live for hundreds and hundreds of years if you accept the apple.

If you refuse her offer, turn to page 106.

If you accept Idunn's apple, turn to page 56.

Once you're safely out of the underworld, you put on the falcon suit and fly into the air. "Follow me to Asgard!" you call to the frenzied crowd below. "The gods need your help!"

They begin to run, and from high above, you lead hundreds of the underworld inhabitants up a rainbow bridge to Asgard.

Odin gasps when he sees them. "Have you lost your mind?" he shouts to you. "What are you doing with all of Hel's prisoners?"

"You'll see," you reply. Then you call to the crowd, "There's an evil witch who's causing trouble here. Will you help me carry her to Midgard?"

"Yes!" they roar.

They rush toward Gullveig and sweep her off her feet. She shrieks and struggles, but the crowd won't let her escape. You fly overhead, guiding the crowd across another rainbow bridge to a remote corner of Midgard. The people put Gullveig down in the middle of a forest. Then they run for the surrounding villages, leaving her behind.

You hover for a moment, listening to Gullveig's howls of despair. "My gold!" she wails. "All the gold I took is still in Asgard, and I know they'll never let me back again!"

Turn to page 53.

As you sail straight ahead you notice that the river runs into a small calm lake. You pull the raft to shore, then walk around the lake, hoping to find the Norns.

Instead, you discover a bubbling well, and beside it the head of a man. There is no blood, no body—just a head. To your shock the blue eyes meet your own and the lips curl into a smile. You try not to scream, but it is the most gruesome sight you have ever seen.

"Don't be frightened," murmurs the head.

"Who—or what—are you?" you whisper with horror.

Turn to page 70.

You must get out of the underworld as quickly as possible. After all, you remind yourself, Odin needs your help. There's no time to waste!

You explore the gloomy caverns around the castle, but finally realize there is only one way out—past the giant wolf! Just thinking about the beast gives you goose bumps!

You retrieve the falcon suit and make your way toward the wolf. The creature is even more gigantic than you remembered. This time you notice that the fur on its chest is matted with blood.

The idea of battling the wolf with your sword makes you tremble with fear. You're tempted to blow the Trumpet of Terror instead. You know it will frighten earthly animals, but this underworld wolf may not be affected at all. Besides, you don't want to call attention to your escape. You have to make up your mind soon—the wolf is staring right at you!

If you decide to use your sword,
turn to page 72.

If you think now is the time to blow the trumpet, turn to page 105.

You race away from the wall of flames, back to Asgard. Thor is still a little dazed when you arrive, and Odin is mad.

"Where's Idunn?" he shouts.

"Never mind Idunn!" you reply. "The fire demons are invading. We barely escaped."

"And only because our friend here blew the Trumpet of Terror and pulled me away from those monsters," adds Thor weakly.

"The fire demons?" gasps Odin. His gaunt face whitens. "Those devils could not have chosen a worse time to attack. Why, without Idunn's apples, we could be killed! And Gullveig! Who knows what she'll do? She may even decide to help the fire demons." He buries his head in his hands.

"What are we going to do?" you ask.

Odin looks up wearily. "I think we should hide."

"Hide?" you shriek. "I thought gods were brave!"

"Gods are only brave when they are immortal," Odin replies sadly. "Without immortality and without courage we are nothing more than human beings with a lot of magic equipment."

Turn to page 58.

You pick up the ax and walk under the scaffolding that supports the ship. Just as you are about to begin chopping the hull, a worker runs up and shouts, "What are you doing?"

"The hull has been constructed all wrong. I have instructions to destroy this section so we can rebuild it correctly. Why don't you find another ax and help me?" you reply.

To your relief the worker believes you. She runs off to get one. You raise your ax over your shoulder and swing it against the hull. The sharp metal blade slices easily through the fingernails. This will be a cinch, you tell yourself.

But after four or five swings of the ax, you notice something strange. The fingernails are growing back!

Before you have a chance to wonder what is happening, strong hands grab you from behind. Looking over your shoulder, you see a woman wearing a wreath of wilted flowers. Half of her face is beautiful; the other half is hideous. You let out a blood-curdling yell, for you know you've been caught by Hel, the queen of the underworld.

Turn to page 71.

You are overwhelmed by the noise and not sure you want to join any army, even Odin's. But just then you see Nils grinning at you from across the table.

"While you were out counting the doors, I learned all about Valhalla," he tells you. "We're immortal now! Every day there's a big battle, but no matter what happens, everyone is healthy and whole again by dinnertime. Come with me, and I'll show you around."

As you listen to the laughter filling the great hall, you decide you are lucky to be in Valhalla.

The End

You turn away from Gullveig and fly back to Odin to return Frigg's falcon suit.

"What an amazing scheme!" exclaims Odin when you arrive. "How can I ever thank you for getting Gullveig out of here?"

You shrug. "Right now, I'm worried about all the people I led out of the underworld. What will happen to them in Midgard?"

Odin puts his hand on your shoulder. "Don't worry. I'll make sure each of Hel's prisoners has another chance at life. Now, tell me: What would you like as a reward?"

You think of everything you've ever wished for, then say, "To tell you the truth I'd like to join Nils and the rest of the crew on the voyage to Iceland. Could you get me on the boat?"

"Nothing could be easier," says Odin. "Let's go!"

The End

As you float down the left branch of the river the clammy green mist envelops you. The vapor smells awful, like rotting food. You notice with panic that the current is becoming fierce. In fact, the water seems to roar. But when you listen carefully, you realize it is not the roar of rushing water, but the ferocious howling of some kind of beast!

Suddenly you find yourself sailing straight toward an enormous winged dragon! The writhing green monster is so long, you can't even see his tail, and his weblike wings could destroy a whole

house with one angry swoosh. You know right away he is Nithog! You remember hearing tales of this dragon when you were little. But, whoever would have thought you'd one day hear his terrifying screeches or smell his foul breath? And you certainly never imagined Nithog would be coiling his powerful body around your raft!

You reach for the Trumpet of Terror, but it is too late. Nithog has already sunk his poisonous fangs into your back.

The End

"All right," you tell Idunn. "I'll take an apple of immortality."

As soon as Idunn hands you one of the golden apples, she retreats to the bottom of the lake. You put on the falcon suit and fly back to Asgard.

"I couldn't find Idunn anywhere," you lie to Odin. "I'm tired and I want to go home."

"But what about Gullveig? Won't you try to lure her out of Asgard?" he asks woefully.

"I'd really rather not," you reply. You are eager to get back to Midgard and find a safe place to hide the apple.

Odin reluctantly takes you down a rainbow bridge to Midgard. You decide not to go home to Sandeborg. You're afraid people will ask why you suddenly chose not to sail to Iceland. You don't want to talk about Odin or your treasured apple, so you settle in a different city.

Amazing changes take place during the 1,048 years that pass since the day Idunn gave you the apple. You witness astounding inventions, from the hot-air balloon to the airplane to rockets. You live to see the first printing press, and then typewriters and computers. You survive the Plague and dozens of wars. Best of all are the holidays; you never get tired of celebrating your birthday.

Finally in 1986 when you eat the last morsel of apple, you decide to write a book about everything that has happened to you. You begin your story in the year 938 when you first met Odin in Sandeborg.

The End

"Why would you want this old trumpet?" you ask the frost giants. "There's nothing special about it at all."

"If it's just an ordinary horn, why won't you give it up?" asks the female giant shrewdly.

"It's all I have," you say, lying. "I'll probably have to trade it for my next meal. Surely you don't want me to starve."

The frost giant acts as if she hasn't heard you. "I don't believe that's an everyday trumpet."

As she begins to pry your fingers from the horn her husband says, "We'll give you the net we use to trap deer. You can catch your dinner with it, or trade it for food."

You aren't happy with the arrangement, but there's not much you can do. The giants take your horn and give you their net.

However, when you see that the net is made of gold, you get an idea! You thank the giants for releasing you and ask for directions to Asgard. Then you hurry back to Odin.

"I have a solution!" You tell Odin breathlessly. "Take me to Gullveig!"

Turn to page 66.

You are stunned. "You can hide if you want to, but I'm at least going to *try* to defend Asgard. Will you help me, Thor? I'll give your belt back to you."

Thor is silent. You follow his gaze to the orange flames leaping around the palaces of Asgard. Odin closes his eye and moans.

"Come on!" you cry, tugging at Thor's arm.

The two of you race toward the fire demons. Gods and goddesses are screaming. Smoke billows from the burning buildings. And before you know what is happening, a demon jumps on your shoulders, flattening you to the ground.

His hot breath scorches the back of your neck. You flail your arms desperately, then reach for the Trumpet of Terror. Just as you lift it to your lips you remember it won't work anymore. You already used it to rescue Thor from the fire demons! Nothing can save you now.

The End

"I'm absolutely not giving up my eye," you tell Mimir. "I'll find the Norns and ask them for help."

"Whatever you choose," says Mimir. "I know a shortcut. Go straight through the valley to the east and you'll come to the Norns."

You thank him and walk toward the valley. But somewhere you take a wrong turn, for you never reach the Norns. Instead, you enter a bleak land where ice covers the trees and a freezing wind cuts through your clothes. Before long you find yourself facing a man and a woman who are twice as tall as any human being. Their skin is encrusted with frost and their fingernails are made of ice.

"How dare you enter the land of the frost giants?" bellows the male giant. Snowflakes spew from his mouth when he speaks.

"I didn't mean to," you explain. "I'm looking for the Norns."

"There's a price to pay for trespassing," scolds the female giant.

You feel her husband's cold fingers encircle your neck. "We want that magic trumpet of yours," he growls.

"This?" you ask, removing the Trumpet of Terror from your belt. The giant's grip prevents you from raising the horn to your lips.

"Yes. Hand it over," snaps the female giant.

If you try to convince the frost giants that it's just an ordinary old horn, turn to page 57.

If you struggle to free yourself from the giant, turn to page 43.

"I'll take my reward in gold!" you exclaim.

"Very well," says Odin. He orders the gods to load three carts with gold.

In your excitement you forget to thank Odin. You can't take your eyes off the crowns and coins and bowls that are shining like the sun. There is so much gold that it takes four horses to draw each cart to Midgard.

You build seven great castles adorned with tapestries and golden chandeliers. You have more servants than you can count. You are so rich, even kings and queens envy your wealth.

But you are not happy. Every night you worry that your gold will be stolen. And every day you find yourself wishing you had still more.

The End

Cautiously you begin to move your arms up and down. You find yourself slowly rising off the ground. You call good-bye to Odin, then beat your wings more forcefully. As you soar through the sky you discover that your eyesight has become so sharp, you can see the color of people's eyes below.

But suddenly you realize you don't know how to recognize Idunn except by her golden apples. While you worry that your search is going to fail, you notice a falcon flying beside you.

Go on to the next page.

"Where are you headed?" it asks.

You are surprised to hear the bird speak. Maybe the falcon suit helps you to understand the language of falcons, you tell yourself. "I'm looking for the goddess Idunn," you reply.

The falcon chuckles in a surprisingly human way. "Come with me. I'll show you."

You need some help, but there's something suspicious about this bird.

"Could you just tell me where she is?" you ask.

"No," replies the falcon, "it's too far away."

If you fly along with the bird, turn to page 8.

If you decide to find Idunn on your own, turn to page 37.

You can't stand the idea of wading back to Asgard through the icy river, so you look around for a rainbow bridge. On the other side of a hill, you spot one. You step onto it carefully, hoping it is the one that leads to Odin. Fortunately it is! You scurry up the bridge, barely noticing the glowing colors.

At the top, Odin joyfully welcomes you back and says, "We'll never be foolish enough to let Gullveig into Asgard again. Thank Yggdrasil, she can't work her evil magic from afar!" Then, noticing your silence, he asks, "Why aren't you happy? You should be proud of yourself."

You shrug sadly. "A giant fish stole the golden boat. I won't get the Trumpet of Terror back unless I return the boat to the dwarfs."

Odin pats your shoulder reassuringly. "Don't worry. I'll send Thor, my strongest son, after the fish. He'll make sure you get your trumpet back."

Sure enough, with his strength-increasing belt, Thor has no trouble getting the boat back. He then visits the dwarfs and exchanges the boat for your Trumpet of Terror.

"Thank you!" you exclaim as Thor hands you the golden horn.

"I told you everything would work out," says Odin. "Now let's go see your reward."

Turn to page 78.

"I have to go to Sandeborg!" you cry. "Please take me back there!"

Although Odin disapproves of your decision, he grabs your hand and rushes to Sleipnir's stable. You leap into the saddle and help Odin mount the horse. Together you race across the rainbow bridge to Midgard. Sleipnir gallops as fast as he can, but the journey seems to take forever.

Odin drops you off on the dock where you first met him. You start to say good-bye, but before the words leave your lips, Odin is hurrying back to Asgard.

You begin shouting at the top of your lungs, "Hurry! There's a tidal wave coming!"

A fisherman looks up from the net he's mending and chuckles. "I tried pulling that same prank when I was a boy."

"I'm not joking!" you shriek. "Run for your life!"

Turn to page 83.

Odin leads you to the witch who is causing all the trouble. Gullveig's eyes glitter cruelly, but after your meeting with the frost giants, you're not afraid.

"I understand you like gold," you tell Gullveig after introducing yourself.

"I love it!" she replies.

"Then perhaps you'll enjoy wearing this golden shawl." You hand her the net the frost giants gave you.

"How beautiful!" says Gullveig. She drapes the net around her shoulders.

"Try putting it over your head," you suggest.

Go on to the next page.

As soon as she does you pull one end of the net, and it closes around Gullveig. She squawks and screams, but she can't get out. She is much too big for you to carry, so you and Odin have to roll Gullveig to the edge of Asgard. There you give her one last shove and she tumbles down a rainbow bridge. Her angry cries grow fainter and fainter.

"Bravo!" shouts Odin. "We'll never let her into Asgard again. I'm sure Idunn will come home as soon as she hears that Gullveig is gone. You've saved us! Now tell me, how can I reward you?"

You shrug, embarrassed by the attention.

"Let me narrow down the choices," says Odin. "Would you like gold or glory?"

If you choose gold, turn to page 61.

If you'd rather be rewarded with glory, turn to page 109.

You are determined to escape from the underworld! You don't want to attract attention, so you hide Frigg's feathered suit between some boulders.

As you search for a way out you try not to listen to the mournful wails of Hel's prisoners that fill the air. You walk all around the solid wall of mountains that surrounds the world of the dead, but you can't find a single passageway. The only way out is past the giant wolf.

Feeling very frustrated, you head for the castle. Near it, you discover dozens of people constructing a massive warship. They are building it with millions of small gray slivers.

"What's this boat made of?" you ask a worker.

"Fingernail clippings from the dead," he answers.

You try not to show your surprise. "What will you use the ship for when it's finished?"

The worker smiles slyly. "Loki will sail in it to Asgard to attack the gods. After the battle, death and evil will rule the universe!"

With a shudder you realize the warship is nearly finished. Although you want to escape as soon as possible to continue your search for Idunn, you wonder if you should try to destroy Loki's warship first.

If you decide to leave the ship alone and continue searching for a way out of the underworld, turn to page 48.

If you want to stay and try to cripple the ship, go on to the next page.

What is the best way to destroy a ship made of fingernails—without getting caught? You stare at the boat for a long time, then look around for ideas.

An ax is lying near the boat. Carefully you run your finger along the edge of the blade. It feels very sharp, certainly capable of chopping a hole in the hull. You stroll casually around the construction, trying to decide if cutting a hole would do enough damage.

Maybe you should try to destroy the entire warship. Using one of the flaming torches nearby, you could burn the boat to the ground! *That* would interfere with Loki's plans! Of course, you'd have to wait for all the workers to go home, and even then it may not be safe. What if there are guards posted at night?

If you try to set the warship on fire,
turn to page 102.

If you think it's safer to use the ax,
turn to page 50.

"I'm what's left of the giant god Mimir since the Vanir gods beheaded me years ago. I'm kept alive with special herbs and the invigorating water of this well. Only rarely do I have visitors. Tell me, what brings you here?"

You explain to Mimir about Gullveig and your search for the Norns.

"You made a wrong turn," says Mimir. "But maybe it was a fortunate mistake, for you've come to the Well of Wisdom. One sip and you'll have all the knowledge you need to solve your problem."

You can't believe it! Immediately you lower yourself to the well.

"Not so fast!" snaps Mimir. "Wisdom is never gained without sacrifice. You must give up one of your eyes before you can taste the magical water."

"Not an eye!" you shriek. You pull back from the well.

"I'm afraid so," Mimir replies. "Even Odin had to give up an eye when he sipped from the well."

You're curious about the Well of Wisdom, but you don't want to lose an eye. You try to think of other ways to solve the Gullveig problem.

If you decide to give up an eye to gain wisdom, turn to page 38.

If you continue to look for the Norns instead, turn to page 60.

"I see what you're doing!" she snaps. She yanks the Trumpet of Terror off your belt. "I *told* Loki live humans cause too much trouble here! Fortunately I have a special island for wretches like you!"

Hel drags you through an icy river to a small island. There she throws you into a dark dungeon crowded with pale, moaning people. To your horror you discover the walls are made of thousands of writhing snakes!

"Make yourself at home," cackles Hel wickedly. "You'll remain here for eternity!"

"Wait!" you cry, but it is too late. She has already disappeared.

The End

You whip out your sword and step toward the giant wolf. But try as you may, you can't get past him. He snarls ferociously and lunges at you. It is all you can do to defend yourself.

Then, out of the corner of your eye, you notice that a crowd has gathered to watch the battle. The moment your attention wanders, the wolf leaps for your throat. Its deadly jaws are wide open. Without thinking, you plunge your sword right into the beast's mouth. Then you let go quickly and yank your hand away.

Go on to the next page.

The wolf groans as it struggles to close its mouth. Your sword is wedged firmly between its jaws.

The people around you begin to cheer. Before you know it, they rush past the wolf. You grab your falcon suit and hurry after them.

Turn to page 45.

Before you've driven more than a few yards, you see several blazing demons leap from the fiery wall. They're running after you! You can already feel the heat from their flaming bodies.

You slap the reins. Toothgnasher and Toothgrinder break into a frenzied gallop. All you can think of is escaping from the fire demons.

Suddenly you feel a horrifying blast of heat. Turning, you see that three demons have jumped into the chariot! You let go of the reins and desperately try to cover your head with your arms. It does no good. Flames surround you and your lungs fill with smoke. Within seconds you are consumed by a scorching orange blaze.

The End

SPLASH! The icy water is so numbing, you can barely move. You float for a moment, paralyzed by the cold. To your shock you see the mammoth fish turn away from the boat and head directly toward you! Frozen or not, you swim to shore as quickly as you can. As you scramble onto the riverbank the fish snaps hungrily at your ankles.

You're safe! You shake yourself dry and watch the fish swim back to the golden boat, where Gullveig is shrieking, "Help! Help! You can't leave me here!" The fish rocks the boat back and forth until Gullveig falls overboard. To your relief she swims to the opposite shore. You're rid of the witch!

But you're not at all happy as you watch the fish propel the golden boat downstream.

"I have to get that boat back!" you exclaim. "The dwarfs will never give me the Trumpet of Terror unless I return their boat! What am I going to do?"

If you follow the fish, you might be able to retrieve the boat, but you're afraid to go near the giant creature again. Besides, you remind yourself that Odin has a reward for you. Maybe you should just return to Asgard and be content with whatever Odin gives you. But somehow you can't stop thinking about the Trumpet of Terror.

If you go after the fish, go on to the next page.

If you head back to Asgard, turn to page 64.

You follow the golden boat as the fish pushes it down the river. You're careful to stay a little behind so the creature can't see you. You're not sure whether fish can hear, but you walk very quietly, just in case.

Before long the fish propels the boat into a smaller stream along the side of the river. There are many reeds growing on the bank, so you have trouble keeping up. Just as you begin to wonder where on earth the fish is going, you see it nudge the boat out of the water onto the shore.

This will be easy, you tell yourself happily. But your excitement soon turns to shock. The fish changes into a red-haired man!

He claps his hands and laughs. "Hah!" he cries, tossing back his head. "Now this boat belongs to Loki!"

You shudder at the sound of the name. All your life you've heard about Loki's sly schemes. Your grandmother used to call him the Father of Lies when she told stories of his evil tricks. You know it won't be easy to get the boat away from him.

Just then Loki spies you through the reeds. "I thought I got rid of you up the river!" he says, glaring at you. "Well, never mind. I'll take care of that!"

The next thing you know, you are a small fish darting through the stream. You have no memory of Loki, Odin, or your life in Sandeborg. All you can think about is finding something to nibble.

The End

Going near the whirlpool might be foolhardy, but you don't want to lose the precious trumpet. You tie a rope around your waist and hand Nils the other end. Before anyone can stop you, you kick off your shoes and leap into the cold green water.

You swim toward the Trumpet of Terror. Just as you reach it a mass of coppery hair swirls all around you. You find yourself tangled in a dense red web! What is it? You struggle to free yourself, but only manage to make the rope slip loose from your waist. Oh, no!

You try not to panic, but you're horrified to find yourself pulled far below the waves. Remarkably, you're able to breathe underwater. You clutch your trumpet and hope for the best.

Turn to page 110.

You follow Odin through the streets of Asgard to a long wharf. There you see a magnificent dragon ship with a red-striped sail. "It's yours," says Odin. "I know you missed your voyage to Iceland to help me get rid of Gullveig. Now you'll be able to sail wherever you like."

You are speechless with delight. A group of gods and goddesses follows you onto the ship. They each take an oar and begin rowing. Grinning happily, you lead the way home to Midgard.

The End

As you board the ship the captain warns you sternly, "No more nonsense, or you'll never sail with me again."

"Yes, sir," you mumble. You take your place by one of the twenty-six oars. Soon the ship glides out of Sandeborg harbor.

By the end of each day your arms ache from rowing, but you are too excited to complain. You gaze at the stars and remind yourself how lucky you are to make this voyage.

It is a stormy day when the captain finally spots Iceland on the horizon. The boat feels dangerously small as the waves toss it from side to side. You and Nils are too seasick to row. You try to distract yourself from your fear and misery by polishing the Trumpet of Terror.

Suddenly you feel the boat lurch violently. The trumpet flies out of your hands and goes overboard into the waves!

"We've been sucked into a maelstrom!" screams Nils.

The ocean whirlpool spins the boat around in dizzying circles. Moaning with terror, the crew clings to the ship. You're scared too, but you never take your eyes off the golden trumpet bobbing in the churning foam.

Go on to the next page.

After several horrifying minutes the maelstrom releases the boat. You find yourself in tranquil waters.

"I can't believe we made it!" cries Nils. When you don't reply, he follows your gaze to the trumpet bobbing on the edge of the whirlpool. "Don't tell me you're upset about losing your horn!" he snaps. "You should be glad we're alive!"

"I know," you answer, "but I can't stand the thought of losing the trumpet. It's so close! If you tied a rope around my waist, I could swim over and get it!"

"You're crazy!" says Nils. "The whirlpool would pull you in!"

If you say, "I'm going to get the Trumpet of Terror back, no matter what," turn to page 77.

If you tell Nils, "You're right. Let's see if the ship is damaged," turn to page 86.

You can't believe it. No one is taking you seriously! They listen to your cries and smile.

Just then, a woman selling fish cries, "Look! The tide is going out!"

Sure enough, the harbor is slowly draining.

"Where is all the water going?"

"It's not low tide!"

"What's happening?"

The people murmur anxiously. You point to the horizon.

There, a tremendous wave is sucking all the water from the shore. The wave grows larger and larger before your eyes!

Dropping their baskets and abandoning their nets, people scurry for shelter. But no one, not even you, can escape. The gigantic wave sweeps over the harbor and through the village, swallowing boats, smashing houses, and drowning every single inhabitant of Sandeborg.

The End

"I'll go straight to the Lapland wizard," you tell Odin. You try not to think about the tidal wave.

Odin places his hand on your shoulder. "I appreciate your help. I'll lend you my enchanted reindeer for the trip."

You help Odin hitch two reindeer to a small silver sled. You climb in. After saying good-bye, you ask, "By the way, how are these deer magical?"

But before Odin can answer, the reindeer are soaring through the air. Cold winds rush past you as you fly to Midgard. Soon you spot the brilliant rugs of the Lapland wizard.

When you land, you find him sitting on a dazzling red rug. He greets you casually as if visitors descend from the sky every day.

Turn to page 92.

You join a group of men examining the ship's battered hull.

"We're taking in water," says the captain. "We'll have to go ashore as soon as possible to repair the damage."

But when you finally reach the shore of Iceland, you find yourselves in a remote and barren region far from the port. There are no villages or trees to be seen, only stark mountains rising out of the dull gray sea.

The captain instructs his brother Erik to take half the crew, including you and Nils, to go for help while the remaining men guard the ship. Being the youngest, you and Nils have to carry the supplies.

"It's not fair," grumbles Nils as the two of you stagger under the weight of the heavy sacks of food.

"Look how far behind we're lagging," you tell him. "I can barely see Erik and the rest of them."

"Well, I can't walk any faster," Nils insists. "You'd think they would wait for us."

You're really not listening to him. You're trying to figure out what smells so strangely. You think it might be smoke, but it's too foggy to see much. You hear a low rumble growing louder. The earth trembles.

Go on to the next page.

You and Nils eye each other fearfully. Then you glimpse the first stream of lava rushing between two mountains.

"A volcano!" you cry. "If we don't catch up with the others right away, we'll be cut off by the lava!"

You try to run.

"We can't outrace the lava!" says Nils. "Look how fast it's coming! Let's go back to the boat."

"But Erik's men need the food we're carrying!" you shout.

With each second, the lava streams closer.

If you grab Nils and try to outrun the lava, turn to page 113.

If you head back to the ship, turn to page 91.

You and Odin manage to carry the boat to Gullveig. She has just toppled over Odin's throne and is chortling with evil delight.

"I've brought you this lovely golden boat for a present," you tell her.

"It's awfully small," she complains, "but the gold is pretty."

"Would you like a ride?" you ask.

Gullveig smiles lazily. "I don't know if I feel like going for a ride just now."

You stand there, dumbfounded, until Gullveig announces, "Well, maybe I *will* take a cruise in that silly little boat after all."

You breathe a sigh of relief. Odin helps you slide the boat into a nearby river. After Gullveig climbs in Odin whispers to you, "This river flows straight to Midgard. Once you're out of Asgard, just get Gullveig out of the boat. Leave her anywhere then sail back here for your reward. Good luck!"

Gullveig sings loudly—and terribly off-key, you notice—as you float down the river. You are busy thinking of ways to get her out of the boat, when suddenly a gigantic fish appears behind you. The fish takes hold of the boat with its powerful jaws and shakes it from side to side.

Gullveig screams so loudly, you can barely think. You're tempted to jump overboard and swim to safety, but the dwarfs won't give you back the Trumpet of Terror if their boat sinks. Maybe the fish will let go if you kick at it.

If you jump overboard, turn to page 75.

If you kick at the fish, turn to page 96.

90

You raise the Trumpet of Terror to your lips, take a deep breath, and blow.

A ghastly sound like a thousand angry screams fills the air. Throughout the many worlds of Yggdrasil the inhabitants pause, gripped by a sense of horror.

But no one is more terrified than the eagle. Its heart freezes dead with fear. You look up just in time to see the great bird fall through the air. It crashes onto the rainbow bridge, crushing you to death.

The End

"The captain is going to be furious when he finds out we got separated from Erik," you say to Nils on the way back.

But you soon discover that the captain has other things on his mind.

The first sign of trouble is a sleek and menacing dragon ship moored near your boat. When you get closer, you see a fierce band of Vikings attacking the remaining members of your crew!

"What's going on?" exclaims Nils.

"Those Vikings must have spotted our trading ship and come to loot it," you answer. "If only I still had the Trumpet of Terror."

"Never mind," says Nils. "We have our swords. Let's leave the food here and go defend our ship."

"Wait. They probably haven't seen us. We could just hide behind this boulder," you suggest.

"What kind of coward are you?" demands Nils.

You sigh. "Our crew is outnumbered. If we go down there, we'll probably be slaughtered."

"We could sneak up on them," says Nils. "We could make all the difference in this battle. I'm going. Are you coming with me?"

If you say, "No, I'm staying right here,"
turn to page 95.

If you tell him, "You're right. I'm coming,"
turn to page 100.

You tell him about Gullveig, then ask, "Could you create a golden rug that would unfurl a bit more with each step she takes out of Asgard?"

"Certainly, but I may not be able to make the rug golden. Would a yellow one like that be all right?" The wizard points to a rug that glows like the sun.

You study the color. "It's *almost* gold, but Gullveig may not like it unless it's *really* gold. Can't you make a golden carpet?"

"I need molten gold to do that. And the only gold I see around here is that horn of yours," he explains. "Would you let me melt it down to make the rug?"

You hate the idea of giving up the Trumpet of Terror to make a golden carpet for Gullveig, but you're not sure she'll be satisfied with a yellow rug.

If you let the Lapland wizard melt down the Trumpet of Terror, turn to page 97.

If you settle for a yellow carpet, turn to page 99.

One of the men on board helps you into the boat. You breathe a sigh of relief.

"How long have you been in the water?" he asks as he wraps his coat around you.

Before you can answer, the boat begins to rock violently from side to side. You look into the ocean to find Aegir's red-haired daughters furiously shaking the ship.

"You can't leave us!" they cry silently.

As the boat flips into the churning waves, throwing the men into the cold sea, you realize sadly that Aegir's daughters are right. You'll never be able to leave their watery kingdom.

The End

You hide behind an enormous boulder while Nils runs toward the battle. You squeeze your eyes shut and put your fingers in your ears. Even so, you still hear the clashing of swords and the cries of wounded men.

The battle is over quickly. When you finally decide to take a look, you see the Viking ship already sailing away. Your shipmates have all been killed.

You turn and run through the highlands. You have no idea where you're going. You just want to get far away.

Hours later you meet an elderly shepherd named Olaf. He brings you home to his small hut and offers you dinner. He listens sympathetically when you tell him about the Vikings

"Stay with me until you feel better," says Olaf.

At first you plan to leave soon, but the days turn to weeks, and the weeks to months. When Olaf dies the next year, you inherit his flock. You spend the rest of your life in that remote part of Iceland, tending your sheep and dreaming about your life in Sandeborg when you still had the Trumpet of Terror.

The End

As soon as your foot strikes the fish, the giant creature thrashes around wildly. Gullveig topples into the water with a splash and quickly swims to shore. At last you're rid of her!

You hold tight to the edge of the boat and kick the fish again. But this time, the fish closes its jaws on your foot. By the time you realize what is happening, it has devoured your whole leg! Your anguished shrieks of horror do nothing to stop the fish from finishing its meal.

The End

You hand the wizard your trumpet and say, "Here, melt it down."

"I'll make your rug tonight in my underground workshop," the wizard tells you. "You can sleep up here on one of my carpets. That purple one is especially nice for dreaming."

You say good night to the wizard and curl up on the purple rug. As soon as you close your eyes you fall asleep. You have fantastic dreams, yet the next morning you can't remember them. All you can think of is the golden carpet the wizard hands you.

"It's beautiful!" you exclaim. "Thank you so much!" You leap into the sled and race back to Asgard.

There you make plans with Odin and his son Heimdall, the god who guards the rainbow bridges, to lure Gullveig out. You place the golden carpet at the entrance to a rainbow bridge to Midgard, then go with Odin to escort Gullveig.

"I've brought you a present," you tell her. "Come see it!"

Gullveig smiles greedily as she stands on the carpet. When she takes a step, the rug seems to grow longer in front of her and shrink behind her. Gullveig laughs gleefully and continues walking on the golden carpet down the rainbow bridge.

You hold your breath, afraid to believe the plan is really working, until Heimdall says, "She's gone for good! Never again will I be foolish enough to let her into Asgard!"

You join the gods in celebration. Tomorrow you'll begin your search for Idunn.

The End

You take a deep breath and blow into the horn. It makes a horrendous noise, a thousand times more frightening than you ever imagined. To your relief the fire demons wither at the sound. Their flames grow dimmer; their grasp on Thor weakens. But Thor, too, is struck with terror. You jump out of the chariot to help him.

"Come on," you say, tugging at his arm.

Thor does not respond. His eyes are wide with horror and his body is rigid. You try to drag him to the chariot, but he is too heavy to budge.

There is only one thing to do. Quickly you unbuckle his belt and put it around your own waist. You don't feel any different, but when you gather Thor in your arms, you discover you can easily pick him up. You carry him to the chariot.

As you take hold of the reins Thor begins to regain his senses. "Th-thank you for saving me," he murmurs weakly. "Where are we going now?"

You're not sure how to answer. Your first instinct is to race back to Asgard to warn Odin about the invasion from Muspellheim. But you know Odin doesn't stand a chance of defeating the fire giants without first taking a bite from Idunn's apples of immortality..

If you tell Thor, "We're going back to Asgard," turn to page 49.

If you answer, "We're going to look for Idunn," turn to page 103.

"I guess a yellow rug would be all right," you tell the Lapland wizard.

"Fine," he replies. The wizard picks up the carpet and explains, "All I have to do is add a few special knots so this rug will magically unroll with each step forward."

You watch intently as he ties a few intricate knots in the rug's fringe. His fingers move so quickly, you can barely see them. Before long the wizard hands you the rug and says, "There! This will work like a dream!"

You climb into the sled and hurry back to Asgard. There you find Gullveig taunting Odin cruelly.

"I'm going to sit on your throne today whether you like it or not! You know perfectly well there's nothing you can do to stop me!" she shouts.

Turn to page 108.

With swords held high you and Nils race toward the Vikings. The battle is swift and brutal. All your shipmates, including Nils, fall dead, and for a moment it is just you against the Vikings. A second later a sword is plunged straight into your heart.

You collapse into the arms of a woman who is wearing a horned helmet and a coat of mail.

"Who are you?" you murmur.

"A Valkyrie," she answers. "I'm taking you to Valhalla."

"Where?"

"Valhalla," she repeats. "All who die bravely in battle go there. You'll join Odin's army."

The next thing you know, you are strong again. You stand on your own two feet facing an immense fortress. The roof is covered with golden shields. You count 640 doors around the building.

Stepping inside, you discover hundreds of warriors feasting and laughing.

"Welcome to Valhalla!" cries one of them. "We've been waiting for you!" He hands you a horn brimming with mead. "Drink up! You deserve it!"

Turn to page 52.

There is no point in lurking around the warship while you wait for the workers to go home. You decide to pass the time by searching near the castle for an escape route. After all, as soon as the ship catches fire you'll have to make your getaway.

You look carefully for signs of an underground passage. You even push aside a few large rocks to see if they hide the entrance to a tunnel. But all you find are three slithery snakes and a web full of hairy spiders. At last you return to the warship.

To your surprise the workers are still busy sawing and hammering even though several hours have passed. You walk up to one carpenter and say, "You work very hard here. When do you get to go home for dinner?"

He stares at you blankly. "Home? Dinner? They don't exist in the underworld. We toil night and day."

"Oh," you reply, trying not to show your surprise.

You figure you may as well start the fire right away. You grab a blazing torch and hold it against the side of the boat. The warship bursts into flame, and the boat explodes with a deafening blast. You fall to the ground. But before you can stumble to your feet, a blazing mast topples onto your back. The flames race over your body. You are doomed!

The End

You drive the chariot through Midgard while Thor peers over the side, looking for Idunn. After a few hours Thor feels strong enough to take the reins. You give him back his belt, then start searching for the goddess.

Just as Toothgnasher and Toothgrinder begin to grunt with exhaustion, you come to a lake glowing in the twilight. In the middle of it you spot a woman with long blond hair that floats on the surface. Twelve golden apples bob around her.

"Look!" you shout over the thunder of the chariot.

"That's Idunn, all right!" cries Thor gleefully.

As the chariot speeds through the water toward Idunn, you grin with pride. Not only did you save the mighty Thor from the fire demons, but you've found Idunn! You hope you'll have as much luck getting rid of Gullveig.

The End

With all your might you blow into the horn.

The only sound that emerges is a weak gurgling. A few bubbles float out of the trumpet. You stare at them with shock and disappointment.

One of Aegir's daughters exclaims, "Look at the bubbles! Let me have that horn!"

She snatches the Trumpet of Terror away. Her sisters swim toward you as the boat sails past. Drat! You'll have to try another time.

The End

You unhook the Trumpet of Terror from your belt and lift it to your lips. You stare into the fierce yellow eyes of the wolf, then take a deep breath and BLOW!

You shudder at the horrible noise that echoes throughout the underworld. To your relief the wolf freezes with panic at the sound.

You run past the beast, but before you have gone three paces, someone grabs you from behind. Long fingernails dig into your sides. You hear hideous laughter.

You find yourself in the clutches of the strangest woman you have ever seen. One half of her face is smooth and beautiful, but the other half is grotesque. On her head is a wreath of dead flowers. A sickening wave of terror washes over you as you realize she must be Hel, queen of the underworld.

"Blow your horn again!" she says, taunting you. "I love that sound! There's nothing more deliciously frightening!"

Hel grips your hand with incredible force and drags you to her dark castle. At the entrance she announces gleefully, "You'll be my official trumpeter. I'll be able to hear the haunting sound of your horn whenever I wish. And I'll be able to keep an eye on you at the same time." Then she tosses her head back and cackles shrilly. Her laughter is a thousand times more terrible than the sound of your trumpet.

How will you ever explain to Hel that you can blow the Trumpet of Terror only once in a lifetime?

The End

"No," you tell Idunn, "I have to bring you back to Asgard. Please come with me."

She sighs. "I suppose that if I don't go with you, Odin will just send someone else. All right, let's go." Idunn gathers her golden apples and swims with you to shore.

You put on the falcon suit and Idunn climbs on your back. She clutches the basket of apples tightly as you fly to Asgard. Along the way you think of a way to get rid of Gullveig. You tell Idunn about your idea.

That night the gods and goddesses of Asgard gather around an immense table for dinner. Gullveig infuriates Odin by sitting in his special chair. You and Idunn—the guests of honor—sit on either side of the witch. Idunn picks sadly at her food.

"What's wrong, Idunn?" asks Gullveig with a sneer. "Aren't you happy to be home?"

Idunn catches your eye, then says, "I did something very foolish. On the way back I spilled all the golden apples. They tumbled down the rainbow bridge to Midgard. I'll have to get them tomorrow."

"Stay right where you are! I'll get those apples myself," snaps Gullveig. She strides out of the dining hall, singing, "Apples so fine, now they're all mine. With apples of gold I'll never grow old!"

Turn to page 114.

When you argue that you want to return to your boat, Aegir and his daughters pretend they don't hear you.

You spend several days playing with his daughters. You don't mind chasing fish and riding waves, but you hate having to overturn passing ships. What's more, you can't get used to being cold and wet all the time. You're determined to escape.

One day a boat sails near the waves that you and Aegir's daughters are riding. It is so close, you think you may be able to climb on board. But you wonder if you can do it without the girls' noticing. Maybe you should blow the Trumpet of Terror to freeze Aegir's daughters, but how would the sound affect the sailors on the boat?

If you decide just to scramble onto the ship,
turn to page 93.

If you lift the Trumpet of Terror to your mouth,
turn to page 104.

Odin looks so miserable that you decide to show Gullveig the rug right away.

"Look at the present I've brought you," you tell Gullveig. You place the rug at the entrance to the bridge.

You hold your breath as Gullveig walks onto the carpet. She takes a few steps. You begin to relax. Odin catches your eye and smiles.

Suddenly Gullveig kicks the rug scornfully and mutters, "Why, this rug isn't made of gold! It's yellow! You can't fool me!" She stalks off the carpet angrily.

Your heart sinks. Odin's smile disappears.

"I'll think of another plan," you tell him with more confidence than you really feel.

Odin just nods sadly. You can tell he's given up hope.

The End

"I'd like glory, please," you tell Odin.

He smiles. "I will create a new nation for you beside your homeland. The forests will be rich with game, and the soil will yield fine harvests. I will make secure harbors for your ships. The people of your nation will be happy and peaceful."

"Thank you!" you exclaim. "That is more than I deserve."

At first the people in your new kingdom question the ability of a leader your age. "We have a mere child on the throne," they complain. "Our ruler is much too young to know how to govern!"

But before long they realize that no one goes hungry in your nation. Even when the harvest is small, you find a way to feed everyone. While other countries send their men to war, your nation is always at peace. "What a wise and generous leader we have!" your people exclaim.

The citizens of neighboring countries notice this too. They ask you to govern their lands as well as your own. Your glory grows greater with each passing year.

The End

Slowly the cloud of red hair separates. You see that it belongs to nine girls who stand before you with a red-bearded giant. They are all shaking with silent laughter.

"What's going on?" you ask the giant, but no sounds emerge from your mouth—only bubbles.

However, the red-haired creatures understand you. And when the giant moves his lips, you *sense* his answer rather than hear it.

"I am Aegir, lord of the stormy seas," he tells you. "My daughters have been complaining that it's too lonely underwater. I told them they should capture a young friend, but I didn't really think they'd be able to find someone their own age. After all, most seafarers are fully grown."

The girls giggle noiselessly.

But Aegir's explanation doesn't seem at all funny to *you*!

Turn to page 107.

The sack feels unbelievably heavy as you and Nils hurry to catch up with Erik. Your back hurts, your legs ache, and your heart pounds wildly.

Out of the corner of your eye you notice that the flowing lava is dangerously close. You drop the supplies you're carrying and shout to Nils, "Let go of your sack! Just run!"

But in his terror Nils trips over your discarded sack and tumbles to the ground. You help him to his feet, then glancing at the approaching lava. You see a blazing red blur, not ten feet away!

"Come on!" You tug at Nils's arm.

He takes one step, wincing with pain. "My ankle!" he cries. "It hurts too much! Go on without me!"

You stand there fearing death, but unable to abandon your friend. By the time you start to run, it is too late. The fiery river of lava swallows Nils, then you.

The End

The gods and goddesses look relieved, but forlorn. "I'm delighted to be rid of Gullveig," says Odin. "We'll certainly never allow her back here. But I do wish we had those apples of immortality."

With a smile Idunn reaches under her skirt and pulls out twelve golden apples. The goddess offers a tiny bite to everyone. "I can hardly believe your plan worked so well," she tells you as she hands you the apple.

Odin raises his cup and shouts, "A toast to our clever friend from Midgard for saving us all!" The gods and goddesses cheer for you. You've never felt so proud!

The End

ABOUT THE AUTHOR

DEBORAH LERME GOODMAN has a BFA in weaving and a graduate degree in museum education. She began writing for children as an education coordinator at the Smithsonian Institution, where her books *The Magic Shuttle* and *Bee Quilting* were published. Ms. Goodman has written two other Choose Your Own Adventure books, *The Magic of the Unicorn* and *The Throne of Zeus*. She lives in Cambridge, Massachusetts, with her husband, John.

ABOUT THE ILLUSTRATOR

TED ENIK is a playwright as well as a children's book illustrator. He has illustrated *The Curse of Batterslea Hall* and *Ghost Hunter* in Bantam's Choose Your Own Adventure series and *The Creature from Miller's Pond, Summer Camp, The Mummy's Tomb, Ice Cave, Runaway Spaceship* in the Skylark Choose Your Own Adventure Series. Mr. Enik is also the illustrator of Bantam's Sherluck Bones-Mystery Detective books. He currently lives in New York City.